STEP INTO READING

3

STEP

READING ON YOUR OWN

HARLEY AT BAT!

by Arie Kaplan

illustrated by Fabio Laguna, Marco Lesko, and Beverly Johnson

Batman created by Bob Kane with Bill Finger

Random House 🏠 New York

Inside a Gotham City jewelry
store, a pair of thieves
held a rare white diamond.
It was as big as a baseball!
Batman was about
to swoop down on
the thieves,
when suddenly—

KA-BOOM!

The wall exploded,

and the villain Harley Quinn

roared in on her motorcycle!

Harley snatched the diamond
from the shocked thieves.

"Ooh, it's sparkly," she said.

Harley laughed

as she spun around

and left through

the hole in the wall.

Batman leaped into
the Batmobile
and chased her!

Batman sped past Harley.
He turned the Batmobile
right in front of her,
blocking her path.

Harley tossed colorful water balloons
at the Batmobile.

She laughed and revved her engine.

The balloons were glitter bombs!
SPLOOSH! SPLOOSH! SPLOOSH!
The Batmobile's windshield
was covered with glittery paint.

Batman couldn't see Harley

as she rode off into the night.

Batman decided to follow
Harley on foot.
A trail of glitter led him
to Gotham City Stadium.

Batman noticed lights
coming from the stadium.
"It's too late for a
baseball game,"
he said.

When Batman reached the stadium,
he couldn't believe what he saw.
Harley had joined the Joker
and his henchmen on the field.

They were all playing baseball—
using the priceless diamond
as the ball!

"Stop right there!" Batman said.

"Sorry!" Harley cried.

"Even you can't stop

the Prankster Playoffs."

"The what?" Batman asked.

"Every year," Harley explained,
"the Joker and I play a ballgame
with a different rare gem—
DUCK!"

The Joker pitched the diamond.
It roared toward home plate.

Batman ducked just in time
as Harley swung her mallet.

THOCK!

Harley hit the diamond
high in the air!
She pushed past Batman
and started running!

The Joker and his goons cheered

as the diamond sailed

into the outfield.

This was Batman's chance!
He used gas to knock out
two of the Joker's goons.

At the same time,

Harley rounded first base.

She did a cartwheel before moving on!

Harley stayed focused on the game.

When she passed second base,

she didn't notice Batman

lassoing the third goon.

Batman looked for the Joker.

The villain had found the gem!

The criminal clown cackled,

"Now, that's what I call

a baseball diamond!"

While Harley rounded third base,
Batman grabbed the Joker.

The hero had caught him off-base!
He quickly tied the villain up.
"Foul ball," the Joker grumbled.

As Harley slid into home plate,
the umpire yelled, "You're OUT!"
Harley shouted, "I'm safe!"

The umpire removed his mask
and held up a pair of Bat-Cuffs.
It was Batman!

Moments later, all the criminals
were tied up on the pitcher's mound.
"It was my turn at bat," Harley pouted,
"until Batman called me out!"